The Rescue Begins in Delaware

Published by Familius LLC, www.familius.com
Familius books are available at special discounts for bulk purchas-
es for sales promotions, family or corporate use. Special editions,
including personalized covers, excerpts of existing books, or books
with corporate logos, can be created in large quantities for special
needs. For more information, contact Premium Sales at
800-497-4909 or email specialmarkets@familius.com

ISBN 978-1-938301-74-2

Printed in the United States of America

Book design by David Miles
Jacket design by David Miles
Illustrations © 2013 by Manelle Oliphant

10 9 8 7 6 5 4 3 2 1

First Edition

The Rescue Begins
in Delaware

CHERI PRAY EARL AND
CAROL LYNCH WILLIAMS

ILLUSTRATIONS BY MANELLE OLIPHANT

familius

Matthew
Stockton

Grandpa
Stockton

Laura
Stockton

Gracie   George

AND KEEP YOUR

EYES PEELED

FOR...

Crowe

Caesar
Rodney

TRACK THE ADVENTURE

 Delaware

A Creepy Message

"Are you sure I can't help?" I said.

Grandpa let out a grunt. "No George. I already told you."

"Ding dang it," I said.

Grandpa sat hunched over his workbench. He glued the cracked seat of an old wooden chair. He can fix anything. That's his job.

I got too close and bumped Grandpa's hand.

"Oops," I said. "Sorry."

Grandpa sighed and wiped glue off his pants. "Will you please let me alone to work, George?" he said. "Why don't you go bother your sister?"

The clock rang twelve times. Midnight. I poked Gracie on the shoulder.

"Hey," I said. "We're up late. Way past our bedtime."

"Duh," Gracie said. "You think so?"

She didn't look at me. She just kept tapping away on an old telegraph machine.

Gracie is nine. So am I. But I'm older than she is by 5.75 minutes. She's taller than me by one and a half inches. But I'm smarter by about 2 feet.

"I'm bored," I said. "Bore-da. Boooored. I want to go home."

She acted like she couldn't hear. So I made faces at her and hopped around like a monkey.

"Stop it," Gracie said. "You're bugging me."

I hopped around even more.

"Sorry kids," Grandpa said. He stretched. "I have to get this done before the museum opens in the morning. Just a little longer, okay?"

"I guess so," I said. I stopped hopping. "Tomorrow's Saturday anyway."

Gracie tapped away.

Tap, tap, tap-tap, tap, tap went the machine.

Our grandpa is the fix-it man at the Stockton Museum of Just About Everything in American

History. That's our family's museum.

Gracie and I have lived with Grandpa for the last two years. Sometimes we come to his shop in the back of the museum after school. And sometimes he lets us help him.

I yawned and peeked over Gracie's shoulder.

"Quit breathing down my neck," she said.

"It would be nice if you could spell out something real," I said. I'm learning about Morse Code in Cub Scouts. So I could tell that Gracie was just tapping gobbledy-gook.

She kept her eyes on the telegraph machine.

"For your information," she said, "this is how people used to talk to each other. Before there were telephones and cell phones."

"I know that," I said.

"And this is my own secret code," Gracie said.

Tap, tap, tap-tap, tap, tap.

I rolled my eyes. "Who are you sending the message to? There's no one at the other end." I held up a broken wire. "It's not even connected."

Gracie didn't answer. *Tap, tap, tap-tap, tap, tap.*

Grandpa looked over. "You two be careful with that machine," he said. "It's no toy."

"All right," Gracie said.

She tapped some more. This time it sounded like real Morse Code.

"Hey," I said. "Good job, Gracie. That was 'S.O.S.' You just made the code for HELP. You know. Three short taps. Three long taps. Then three more short taps."

Gracie pulled her hand back like something bit her. She looked at me. Then she stared at the machine.

"I'm not doing it," Gracie said. She shook her head.

taptaptap Tap—Tap—Tap taptaptap

"But it can't do that by itself," I said. "Can it?"

"What's going on?" Grandpa said. He walked over.

"I don't know," Gracie said. "The machine started working on its own."

The three of us were quiet.

But the machine went on talking. *taptaptap Tap—Tap—Tap taptaptap*, it said, which means "SOS—HELP."

Gracie touched her silver locket. It used to be Mom's. Gracie always touches that locket when she's nervous.

I pushed my glasses up. I was creeped out.

"You kids move away," Grandpa said. We stepped back and he sat down in front of the telegraph machine.

"The wires are cut," I said, and shivered.

"They've been cut for more than a hundred years," Grandpa said. He rubbed at his chin.

"Maybe we should leave," Gracie said. "You know. Go home."

"Good idea," I said. I headed for the door.

"Shhh," Grandpa said, holding up his hand. He narrowed his eyes and listened.

taptaptap Tap—Tap—Tap taptaptap

Then the tapping changed. A new message was coming. But I couldn't understand it.

Grandpa pointed to his desk. I saw his hand shake. "Grab a pencil and some paper, George. Quick."

"What's happening?" Gracie said. Her eyes bugged out.

I ran to Grandpa's desk. His notepad and pencil were lying there.

"Here." I gave them to him. My heart thumped.

Grandpa wrote the words down. "Delaware . . . 1776. . . . Trapped. . . . Please . . . help," he said out loud.

Then he dropped the pencil.

"What's wrong?" I said.

Gracie pulled at his sleeve. "Grandpa?" she said in a small voice.

"Matthew and Laura," Grandpa said.

"What?" Gracie said. "You mean Mom and Dad?"

Grandpa nodded.

My stomach got all Jell-o-y. *Mom and Dad?*

But it couldn't be them. They disappeared from right here in the museum two years ago.

And they never came back.

CHAPTER 2

A Late Night Visitor

The telegraph stopped tapping.

"Answer them," I said. My voice went all high with excitement. "Before they go away." I squeezed Grandpa's arm.

"I will, Gracie," Grandpa said. "I will."

George nodded. "Hurry up, Grandpa."

Grandpa tapped out a message.

"What are you saying," I said. "Tell them we miss them. Tell them to come home. Right now."

Grandpa clicked away on the telegraph. Then he sat back.

We waited for an answer.

But the machine wouldn't work now. Not at all. There was no sound in the shop.

Me and George stood there. And stared at Grandpa.

"Delaware," Grandpa said. I could tell by looking at him he was thinking hard. "Trapped in Delaware?"

Grandpa walked to a map of the United States. It hung on the wall by his desk. There were red lines drawn in every state on the map.

He ran his finger over the marks.

"Oh," Grandpa said. He frowned. "Look kids." He pointed to the state of Delaware.

"Whoa—what's that?" George said. He took a step and tripped over a stool.

George is a klutz.

On the map, the word "Dover" blinked off and on like a light.

"Why is it doing that?" I said. My voice was a whisper.

I stood next to Grandpa and stared at the map.

"I think," Grandpa said, "your mother and father are in Dover right now. And they're lost.

George touched the light like it was hot.

"But they said they're trapped," I said. "So are

they lost or are they trapped?"

Grandpa nodded. "Trapped," he said. "And lost. At the same time."

"Then they need help," George said. "Call the police."

"But they sent us a message from Dover, Delaware," I said. "So *they* must know where they are. Right?"

"So they, *aren't* lost?" George said. He looked confused.

I *felt* confused.

Grandpa rubbed his hands over his face. "I have something to tell you two. Sit down."

Right then there was a knock at the museum door.

Grandpa's head jerked up. He looked at George and me.

I touched my necklace. My heart pounded.

George pushed his glasses up.

The knock sounded again.

"Who could that be?" Grandpa said. "It's so late."

"The museum's closed," George said. "So maybe . . . " He stopped talking and his eyes went wide. "So maybe it's Mom and Dad."

It was hard to breathe.

"Grandpa?" I said.

Together we ran to the front of the museum. Me and George and Grandpa.

I pushed past George so I could get there first.

"Quit it, Gracie," he said.

But I had to see Mom and Dad. It had been so long. I missed them both so much.

Through the dark rooms to the front of the museum we ran. Past the carousel horse. Past the giant photograph of Robert E. Lee. Past the dishwasher in the 1950s kitchen exhibit. Only the glow on the exit signs showed us the way.

Grandpa fell behind.

"Don't open that door," he said. His voice echoed through the rooms. "Gracie? George?"

But it was too late.

Me and George ran through the black curtains. And into the front entry of the museum.

I stood at the door trying to open the three locks.

George slapped at my hands. "Let me do it," he said. "I'm faster."

"Don't," I said.

"Wait, kids!" Grandpa said from behind us.

The last lock clicked. I threw the door open wide.

A tall, thin man stood in the doorway. His face

was dark in the shadows.

I looked past the man, out into the parking lot.

No Mom and Dad. They weren't home after all.

Tears stung my eyes. I sniffed.

George squeezed my hand.

"Good evening," the man said. He wore an old time-y hat. And an old time-y coat. And he carried a cane with a silver handle.

Grandpa flipped on the light.

"I've been waiting to meet you, children," the man said. He smiled at us and made a little bow.

"Crowe," Grandpa said.

The man tipped his hat. I saw that his hair was blacker than the sky outside. And his eyes were smoke gray.

"Michael," he said, calling Grandpa by name. "It's been a long time."

Grandpa moved me and George behind him. "Go back to the shop," he said to us.

George didn't go.

Neither did I.

Crowe's lips went thin. His gray eyes narrowed.

"Nah, we better stay here with you," George said. He peered out from behind Grandpa.

But Grandpa, who never gets mad at us, said,

"Go back to the shop, George. Gracie. I mean it."

I backed up a little.

Crowe stepped into the room.

"You're not welcome here, Crowe," Grandpa said. Then he looked at George and me again. "Go *now*," he said. His voice made me jump.

And so we left. Sort of.

We walked through the curtains. But we didn't go back to the shop.

"Let's wait here," I said to George, "and watch."

George waited beside me. "Yeah," he said. "In case Grandpa need us."

We parted the curtains and peeked out. I nodded toward Grandpa and Crowe. "Who is that guy?"

"I'm not sure," said George. "But I have a bad feeling about him."

"I told you never to come here, Crowe," Grandpa said. He sounded angry. "You want me to call the police?"

Crowe let out a little laugh.

"And say what, Michael? That a man from the *past* is stalking you?"

Grandpa sighed and leaned against the doorway. He seemed tired. And not just from staying up late fixing chairs.

"George," I said. "What's going on?"

George held a finger to his lips.

"You already know," Crowe said. "We've been over this many times."

Grandpa straightened up a little.

"Yes we have," he said. "And you know my answer. No exchanges. None. Not until my daughter and son-in-law are home safe. Not until my grandkids have their parents back."

"A little bargain, Michael," Crowe said. "You give me the machine. I'll help you get Matthew and Laura home."

I nudged George. "What machine?" I whispered.

George shrugged. "How should I know?"

We waited for Grandpa to answer.

I wanted to shout, "Do it, Grandpa. Give him whatever he wants." But instead I said nothing.

I just listened.

CHAPTER 3

A Time *What?*

I couldn't see Grandpa and Crowe. Gracie was right in front of me. What was Grandpa doing? And why wasn't he answering?

I shifted around a little so I could see around Gracie's head.

"Stop moving, George," Gracie said. "I'm trying to listen.

"I can't see," I said back.

"Do you want Grandpa to know we're still here?" Gracie said. "He'll make us leave."

"Shh, " I said. I shoved Gracie over. She shot me a dirty look. But now I could see a lot better.

Grandpa still would not let Crowe inside.

"No deals, Crowe," Grandpa said. "I don't trust you. At all. And Laura and Matthew shouldn't have trusted you either."

"Now Michael, you know none of that was my fault," Crowe said.

Grandpa snorted.

"This would work out well for both of us," Crowe said. "I help you. You help me."

"And how do you plan to help me?" Grandpa said.

"I can bring Laura and Matthew back to you. Isn't that what you want?"

"You tried that before," Grandpa said. "You brought them back all right. A hundred years too early."

Gracie let out a gasp. "Did you hear that, George? He can bring Mom and Dad home."

I felt my eyes go wide. "He said a hundred years too early. What does *that* mean?" I said.

Gracie shook me. "Are you listening to me, George? Crowe says he can save our parents."

"Sh-h-h," I said. I didn't want to miss another word.

"I think I've worked out the . . . small problems,"

Crowe said.

"Please let him be able to get Mom and Dad back," Gracie said. She kept her voice low.

I stared at her. Her skin was a little green. From the exit sign light above our heads. And her eyes were a little shiny from almost-tears. I felt bad, too. I missed Mom and Dad even more.

"Let me help you, Michael," Crowe said. His voice was smooth. Like caramel candy.

"You can't," Grandpa said. "You'll get yourself and that blasted machine stuck in time, too. Like you did Matthew and Laura."

Gracie squeezed my arm. Her nails pinched.

I looked at her. She looked at me.

"Mom and Dad are . . . stuck? In time?" I said. What in the heck?

Then Crowe grabbed Grandpa's shirt.

I got ready to jump out and help Grandpa.

But Grandpa knocked Crowe's hand away.

"Listen, old man," Crowe said. His voice was a growl. "I know they've contacted you. And I know that you're going to use the time machine. Tonight."

The time *what?*

Gracie squeezed my arm harder.

I leaned forward so I could hear better.

"No one's going anywhere in that thing," Grandpa said. His voice got loud. "*No one.* Not you. Not me. Not . . . "

"Your grandchildren?" Crowe said.

"Never. I will not allow it."

"What do they mean, George?" said Gracie.

"I think I know," said George. "But I don't believe it."

Grandpa did something I've never seen him do before. He got right in Crowe's face.

"Leave, Crowe," Grandpa said. "I mean it."

Grandpa pushed the door. He tried to close Crowe out of the museum.

"Don't ever come back," Grandpa said.

"Listen to me, Michael." Crowe stuck his foot in the door. "George and Gracie are the only ones who can save your family. After all, they never did anything wrong. Not like you and me."

"Now you're asking me to risk trapping George and Gracie, too." Grandpa's voice was loud. "And I won't do it."

"Be reasonable. Once I help you get Laura and Matthew home," Crowe said. "I'll take the time machine off your hands. No more problems for you."

Grandpa closed the door in Crowe's face.

Then he snapped off the light.

The room went dark.

I heard Grandpa lock the three locks.

I heard him let out a sigh.

I heard Gracie thump my head with her knuckles.

My glasses hopped down my nose. "Ow," I said. "Why did you do that?"

"Let's go," Gracie said. "We've got to get back to the shop before Grandpa does. We don't want him to know we spied on him."

She disappeared down the black hallway.

I followed her.

I couldn't stop thinking.

Time machine? What was that all about?

First that message. Then Grandpa's worried face.

Now Crowe. And all strange things Grandpa said. *Trapped. A hundred years before. Time machine.*

Crowe got Mom and Dad trapped? The idea made my insides wobble.

Gracie and I burst into the shop. We plopped onto two chairs and waited for Grandpa.

Gracie's face was white. Like an egg shell.

"Act natural," I said. "You look scared. Like you know something."

"So do you," Gracie said. She rubbed her cheeks and smoothed her hair.

"Gracie, Crowe was talking about a time machine," I said.

"That's impossible, George," Gracie said.

Grandpa stepped into the room.

"I know you two heard," he said. "I saw both of you, glowing green under the exit sign." He held out his hands. "We have to talk, kids."

Gracie nodded.

"Okay." I waited for him to say something.

Grandpa sat on his desk. He didn't look comfortable.

After a minute he said, "Remember when your mom and dad . . . disappeared?"

"Yeah," I said. "That was THE worst day of my

whole life." I still have bad dreams about it.

"I remember, too," said Gracie. Her face still had that egg shell color.

"Well, they didn't *exactly* disappear," Grandpa said. Then he stopped and looked away. "They got lost in time."

"I knew Mom and Dad wouldn't leave us for no reason," said Gracie.

""I was right," I said. I was so excited I jumped off my chair. I had to walk around. "They're trapped, like in a time warp."

"Yes," Grandpa said. "In a way."

"They got lost in a time machine," I said. "It's Crowe's time machine, isn't it? But why did he come . . . "

I stopped. Just like that, I knew why Crowe had come tonight. That time machine was, *here*. Somewhere in our family's museum.

"It's not possible," Gracie said. "That stuff only happens in the movies. Or in books. This is real life."

Grandpa shrugged. "Your mom and dad got mixed up with Crowe. And he showed them the time machine." Grandpa took a deep breath. "He needed them to take him back to his own time. In the late 1800s."

"I don't understand. Why didn't they take him?" I said.

"They didn't trust him, that's why," said Grandpa. "And neither should you."

"Couldn't Crowe take himself home?" Gracie said.

Grandpa shook his head. "I guess not. I don't know how that all works. And he won't tell me. So I think he must have done something awful. Which is why he can't get home without help."

"Where's the time machine now?" I said. It had to be in the museum somewhere. Otherwise, Crowe wouldn't be snooping around here.

Grandpa stared hard at me and Gracie. "I won't tell you," he said.

"Why not?" I said.

"Because it's dangerous. That's why not," Grandpa said. "And because I said so."

I hated that answer.

"But Grandpa, we could use it to get Mom and Dad home," Gracie said. "We could ask Crowe to help. He said he would."

"Even if he would help us, he can't," Grandpa said.

I looked around the room. Where would Grandpa hide a time machine?

I peeked inside an old cabinet. I opened a big trunk. Then I looked at the old telephone booth. Grandpa never let me or Gracie near it. He yelled at me the one time I tried to step inside.

And Grandpa never yells.

I moved closer to the telephone booth.

"George," Grandpa said, "Stop poking around. You won't find it."

Drat. I didn't think he was paying attention.

I stopped. Until Grandpa looked away again.

Grandpa walked over to Gracie. He touched her hair.

"Crowe's the reason your parents disappeared. He didn't tell us that could happen. And he knew. You can never trust him."

Grandpa took out his handkerchief and wiped his forehead. "Besides, I don't think the time machine likes Crowe. It won't help him."

The telephone booth was a tall box made of wood. Except for the door. And that was partly glass. It didn't look like a time machine. But it had to be.

Grandpa and Gracie stopped talking. The room was dead quiet.

Then came the, *tap, tap tap* of the telegraph.

"It's them!" Gracie said. "It's Mom and Dad.

CHAPTER 4

The Black Hole

"We have to help them, Grandpa," I said. "We have to help Mom and Dad." For a minute I thought I might cry.

George didn't say anything. He leaned inside the old telephone booth. Grandpa would be real mad if he saw that.

But Grandpa didn't see George.

"He grabbed a pencil and jotted down words. "Crowe . . . is . . . looking . . . for the . . . time machine."

Then the telegraph went quiet. Grandpa saw George.

"George!" he said. "Get out of there."

I jumped. I could feel my heart in my throat.

George jerked back so fast he conked his head on the side of the booth. His glasses bounced off his face and fell on the floor.

"What's the matter, Grandpa?" I said. "It's just an old telephone booth."

Then I knew. And I knew George knew, too.

"This is the time machine," George said. He picked up his glasses and put them back on. "That's why you won't let me and Gracie near it."

George touched the phone booth again.

"Stay away from that," Grandpa said. He grabbed George by the shoulders. "It's dangerous. One foot inside and you might disappear. Like your parents."

George's eyes almost popped out of his head.

I stood up, but my legs trembled. So I sat back down.

"Grandpa, please," I said. "Tell us what's going on."

Grandpa sighed.

"You've found the time machine," he said. "So you might as well know everything. George, sit down by Gracie."

George sat down beside me. Grandpa did, too.

"You remember what your parents' jobs were, right kids?" Grandpa said.

"Sure," I said. "They bought antiques for the museum."

Grandpa nodded. "Right. They picked up the time machine at an auction. Of course, they didn't know it was a time machine at first. At the time it looked like a bathtub. One of those old jobs with claw feet."

"But it's a phone booth," I said.

"Right. You never know what it's going to be," Grandpa said. "It changes shape when it travels. I'm not sure why."

"I don't get how you'd ride around through time in a bathtub, Grandpa," said George. "Wouldn't you fall out?"

I rolled my eyes. "Hush, George," I said. "We've moved on."

"When your mom and dad met Crowe," Grandpa said. "I had a bad feeling about him from the start. But he showed Laura and Matthew how to travel through time. We were all amazed, but excited."

"Why did Crowe give Mom and Dad the time machine?" said Gracie.

"I didn't know then, but I found out later that he needed them," Grandpa said. "I don't think he can get home to his own time without help. He was using them. They didn't know."

Grandpa ran his hand along the arm of an antique sofa. "Your parents found such great pieces for the museum."

"You mean Mom and Dad went back in time to *buy* stuff?" George said.

"Yes," Grandpa said. "They brought a lot of items back. Almost a whole museum full.

"And now they're in trouble," George said.

"We have to do something," I said. "We can't leave Mom and Dad out there." I didn't even know where "out there" was. I felt for my locket.

George rubbed his temples. He had one of his big ideas. I could tell.

"Grandpa, do you have a list of the stuff Mom and Dad bought?" George said. He sounded bossy. More like my smarty-pants brother.

"I do," Grandpa said. He went to a drawer and pulled out a thick bunch of papers.

"That is a lot, " I said, surprised.

Grandpa nodded. "They were excited. So was I."

"Wait a minute," George said. "What do you

mean, 'we'?"

"Did you bring things home with you, too, Grandpa?" I said. I couldn't believe it. Grandpa had traveled in time.

"I'm afraid so," Grandpa said. "We didn't know we broke the rules of time."

George jumped up. "What if we take it all back?" he said.

"Us?" I said. "Like me and you, George?"

"Yes," said George. "How about it, Gracie?"

"You mean . . . if we take everything back—"

"—maybe Mom and Dad can come home." George finished my sentence.

Grandpa looked at us. "You two aren't going anywhere," he said. "And *I* can't go. I traveled with your parents a few times. I brought stuff back, too, remember?"

"Why weren't you trapped, Grandpa?" I said.

He shrugged. "I don't know. I didn't go as often. I stayed with you kids. Maybe that's why. But I might not be so lucky next time."

"You mean you could get stuck in time, too?" I said. I felt cold all over.

Grandpa nodded. "And if I get trapped, the two of you will be all alone."

Me and George were quiet for a long minute.

I thought of Mom and Dad. I thought of how people always said we had the best museum ever.

"So we can't do anything to help them?" I said.

"We can't just leave them in Delware," said George, "forever."

Grandpa didn't say anything. And neither did I. But I thought how awful it would be if Grandpa disappeared, too.

It was then that we heard the noise. Someone was in the museum with us.

"Michael?" It was a man's voice.

"Crowe," Grandpa said. He jumped up. "He's in. He's broken into the museum."

"He'll find the time machine," George said.

"That's not all he's after. Stay here," Grandpa said. "Do not leave this room. And do not make a sound."

"Shouldn't we call the police?" I said.

But Grandpa was gone.

"Hurry, Gracie," George said.

"Hurry what?" I said.

"Look through that stack of papers," George said. "Find out what Mom and Dad bought in Delaware."

"Dover, Delaware," George said. "That's where they are right now. That's where their message came from."

I ran my finger down a page.

"Two school desks with benches," I said. "1776."

In the background I could hear Grandpa and Crowe talking. Their voices were loud.

"I know where those desks are," George said. "Stay here."

"George, wait," I said. I grabbed his sleeve. "Grandpa said that Crowe doesn't want the time machine. So, what does he want?"

He stared straight into my face. "He wants us, Gracie," George said.

Then he rushed from the room.

Now I could hear what Grandpa was saying. "No deal, Crowe." he said.

The spit dried right up in my mouth. I pulled on my necklace.

In a moment, George backed into the room, dragging two school desks with him. The legs screeched on the floor.

"I gotta get the rest," he said and ran out again.

When George came back, he had two benches. He pulled them and the desks in front of the phone booth.

"Done," he said. "Help me shove them in, Gracie."

George and me tried to push the desks into the phone booth. But they wouldn't fit.

"How does this thing work?" George said. "These are way too big."

George leaned on a desk. "I need to think."

I leaned on the desk next to him.

The time machine trembled.

I stepped back. George stepped forward.

"Let's try something," George said. He sat on one of the benches.

The time machine rattled hard. The doors cracked open.

"I think it wants us to go," I said. "But I'm scared, George."

"Come on, Gracie," George said. "We have to do this. "We have to help Mom and Dad."

"I know," I said.

So I sat on the other bench.

Now the desks shook, too.

The shop door burst open.

"George!" Grandpa said, running into the room. "Gracie!"

I looked over my shoulder. Grandpa ran toward us. Crowe was right behind him.

The time machine made a loud whirring sound. Like a helicopter. And lit up. A bright glowing light.

George smiled. "It's working," he said.

A gust of hot wind hit our faces.

"That's mine," Crowe said. His voice was a shout. "You can't go without me."

"Stay away from them," Grandpa said. He grabbed Crowe's arm.

Two pair of seatbelts grew out from under the benches and snapped together over our laps.

The window of Grandpa's shop blew open. Papers flew in the air.

Then the time machine opened up wide like a mouth. All I could see was swirling darkness.

"George," I said. "I think I changed my mind."

"Me, too," George said.

Crowe took hold of my school desk and pulled. But the time machine pulled harder. I slid across the floor to the black hole.

"Wa-a-aits!" I said.

The hole swallowed me and George. And the desks. And the benches, too.

Then *zoom*! We were inside the time machine.

CHAPTER 5

Gracie to the Rescue

"I smell a horse, George," Gracie said. She gave a loud sniff.

My head spun. I felt dizzy.

"Yeah, well. That's not all I smell," I said. I held my nose. "If we're in Dover, it sure does stink."

I looked over at Gracie.

A big black horse stared back at me.

I screamed.

The horse screamed, too.

"Get away from me," I said. I fell off my bench and rolled outside. "Help! A fat smelly horse is sitting on my sister."

I turned around. The time machine was right there behind me. But it didn't look like a telephone booth anymore. It looked like an outhouse.

An outhouse? Yuck.

The horse peeked at me. "Where's the fat smelly horse?" it said.

I blinked. "You can talk?"

"No duh." The horse pawed at a huge silver locket hanging from its neck.

I blinked and looked again. "Gracie—is that you?"

"Of course." The horse squinted at me. "What are you wearing, George? You look ridiculous."

I looked down at myself. I had on tights and short, brown, itchy pants. And . . .

"Wait a minute," I said. "*Tights*?"

Gracie the horse giggled. The giggle turned to a neigh. Her eyes went wide.

"Something is wrong," she said. She turned her long neck and looked back at her rump. "This is not right."

"I'll say," I said. "I'm wearing tights."

Gracie trotted close and put her long face in mine. Her flappy lips moved when she said, "Tights, schmights. I'm a horse."

She had a point.

"A horse with bad breath," I said. I waved my hand in front of my nose. "Back up, please."

"I should step on you," Gracie said. She lifted a hoof.

"I think Grandpa forgot to tell us a few things about time travel," I said.

"You think?" Gracie said. She sounded grumpy.

"Wow," I said. "How are you doing that? Is this a costume or are you the real thing?" I opened her mouth and looked inside.

Gracie chomped down. But I moved my hand in time.

"Hey," I said. "You almost bit my fingers off."

"Be polite, George," she said. "And remember that I'm way bigger than you."

I stared into her nostrils. "Boy, that's the truth," I said.

Gracie gave me a nudge. "Stop messing around, George. We've got work to do."

I looked around. We had landed in the backyard of a small white house. Tall trees grew close to the yard. Plus there were tree stumps all over. The air around us felt hot and sticky.

"Listen," Gracie said. Her ear twitched.

I heard people shouting from somewhere near-by.

"What's that?" I said. "A baseball game? Did people play baseball in 1776?"

Gracie nodded, like horses on TV do. "It's coming from over there."

The crowd noises got louder.

"Let's find out what's going on," Gracie said. Then she let out a little whinny. "Mom and Dad might be there."

"Right," I said.

We tip-toed around the corner of the house. Well, I tiptoed. Gracie clomped.

"George." Gracie bumped me with her nose. She almost pushed me over. "I think this house is a school." Her horse-y voice sounded excited. "Do you see that sign?"

I looked at the front of the house. A sign on the gate read, "Master Pritchard's Common School." A bell hung from the rail on the porch. "It is a school, Gracie," I said. "And I bet this is where Mom and Dad got the desks."

"I'll peek in the windows and check for clues. You put the desks on the porch," Gracie said. "Then we'll find Mom and Dad and get back to Grandpa.

Easy."

"How about *I* look in the windows and *you* move the desks?" I said. "You're bigger."

"You think I can do that with these?" Gracie waved a hoof in front of my eyes. "I have no fingers."

"I see that," I said.

I dragged the first desk onto the porch. But I tripped on the way up the steps and banged my shin.

"Ouch!" I said. "This isn't so easy, you know."

"Don't be a whiny baby," Gracie said. She walked to a window.

"No one's in there," she said. "This is the smallest classroom I have ever seen, George. There are tiny desks and benches in it."

I dragged the second desk toward the porch. Gracie whinnied at me.

"Come over here, George. Quick."

"You want . . . to help me . . . with this . . . first?"

She didn't move. Just stood at the edge of the porch, staring at something. If she had been a hunting dog, she would have pointed.

"What's the matter?" I said.

"Look over there," she said. She tipped her nose up. "Across that big field."

I looked out onto a field of grass. A dirt road ran around it. Mr. Pritchard's school sat on one edge of it. Next to the road I saw a church and some other wooden buildings.

"Wow. Dover isn't a very big town, is it?' I said. "No cars or buses or anything. And hey, that field must be the Village Green. Remember, Gracie?" I said. "Like on the drawing of Boston. In the museum."

But Gracie wasn't really listening to me. She nodded. "That's where all that noise is coming from."

A small crowd of people had gathered in front of a red brick building. The building stood near the Village Green. The people hollered at a man on the steps above them. They sounded angry.

"What's going on?" I said. "Do you see Mom and Dad?"

"No," Gracie said. "Check out how everyone is dressed, though. Like the people in our history books. You know, the chapter on . . . "

"On the Revolutionary War?" I said.

Gracie looked at me.

I looked back at Gracie.

"War?" she said.

Gracie was right. The men all wore tights. And

the women wore long dresses and caps on their heads. The guy on the steps had a green scarf over his nose and mouth.

He held up his hands to quiet the crowd. "The prisoners will remain in jail until they have a trial," he said in a loud voice.

My heart sped up.

"Maybe that's what Mom and Dad meant when they said they were trapped," I said to Gracie. "They're in jail."

Gracie whinnied and stomped. "Mom and Dad in jail?" she said.

"You can't do that, Mr. Rodney," someone in the crowd said.

"These men are Tories," Mr. Rodney said. "They're on the side of the British."

The people got real loud now. Someone threw a rock. It hit Mr. Rodney in the shoulder.

That made me jump back. "Whoa," I said.

"Poor Mr. Rodney," Gracie said. "He better run." She pawed the ground.

"The Colonies must be free from British rule," Mr. Rodney said. He held his shoulder like it hurt. "We will fight for our freedom if we have to. You may not join us, but you cannot stop us."

"Our guns will stop you," a man said.

I caught my breath and grabbed at Gracie. I got a handful of mane.

"We're in Delaware all right," I said. "Right before the Revolutionary War."

"Oh great. Oh great. Oh great," Gracie said. "Did they shoot horses in the Revolution?"

She paced. If a horse can do that.

"How should I know?" I said. "Besides, you're not going to the Revolution. We have to break Mom and Dad out of jail."

"Why didn't they choose a safer time to come to Dover?" Gracie said.

I was thinking the same thing. Twins do that sometimes.

"Now we're right in the middle of trouble, too," I said.

"This is terrible." Gracie touched her locket with her hoof. Her horse-y face looked all worried.

Another rock sailed toward Mr. Rodney. It almost hit his head.

More people picked up rocks.

Bad. Bad, bad, bad.

"Is Mr. Rodney one of the good guys?" Gracie said.

"He's on the back of the Delaware quarter," I said. "So I guess he is." I collect state quarters. Sort of. When I don't spend them on candy.

"Then why did he throw our parents in jail?" Gracie said. She was getting grouchy again.

I shrugged. "How should I know?

"We need answers right now. From that Mr. Rodney guy." Gracie knelt down. "Get on my back, George."

"Are you crazy?" I said. "Those people have rocks." I didn't budge. "And they're throwing them."

Mr. Rodney tried to calm the crowd. But the people moved closer to him. They yelled and shook their fists.

"*Now*, George." Gracie used her bossy sister horse-y voice.

I was more afraid of Gracie than getting hit in the head with a rock.

"Oh, all right. Keep your tail on." I climbed onto her back and grabbed a fist full of mane.

"Stop pulling my hair," she said.

Gracie jogged. Or trotted. Or whatever. But she was bouncing my brains loose.

"Can't . . . help . . . it," I said.

Then she charged us through the crowd of angry people. Up the steps of the building we went. Straight to Mr. Rodney. Gracie stopped but my stomach kept trotting.

"Get that horse out of here," a man said. He smacked Gracie's rump.

Gracie jumped forward. She gave the man an evil look.

"Get on, Mr. Rodney," Gracie said.

Mr. Rodney looked at me. He spoke through the green scarf that covered his mouth. "What did you say, boy?"

"Nothing," I said. "That was my sister."

Gracie gave my leg a nip.

"Ouch," I said. "I mean, would you like a ride, Mr. Rodney?"

Mr. Rodney looked at the crowd. He dodged another rock. Then he climbed on Gracie's back. Right in front of me.

"Go, girl," he said. He tapped Gracie's sides with his heels.

Somebody grabbed my ankle. I looked down.

It was Crowe. Right here in Dover, Delaware. Dressed like everyone else.

He smiled and his gray eyes narrowed. "George

and Gracie," he said. His words hissed like a snake.

My stomach went cold.

Crowe pulled on me. But I kicked his hand away.

"Hurry Gracie," I said. "It's Crowe. Go."

I wrapped my arms around Mr. Rodney's waist and held on tight.

Gracie whinnied. She lifted up on her back legs and pawed the air.

"Don't let them get away," Crowe hollered.

But he was too late. Gracie was a fast horse, for a girl.

In a flash we were gone.

CHAPTER 6

The Mysterious Mission

I ran as fast as I could. No matter what they tell you, being a horse is not as easy as it looks.

I felt Mr. Rodney slump against my neck. We ran through the grassy field, past some houses, and through a wooded area.

"Hey," George said to Mr. Rodney. "Are you okay?"

Is he dead, George?" I said. I slowed down to a trot.

"My illness has caused me to imagine that a horse is speaking to me," Mr. Rodney said. "I'm hearing things. I must take to my bed."

Uh oh. I had to remember to keep my horse mouth shut when George and I were around other people.

"Are you sick?" George said.

"I am, boy," Mr. Rodney said. "If you can take me home, I'll trouble you no more."

"Tell Gracie where you live, Mr. Rodney," George said. "You can drive a horse better than I can."

"Very well," Mr. Rodney said. "Straight on, Gracie."

He grabbed hold of my mane and held me steady. Mr. Rodney was for sure a better driver than George.

The sun beat down on us as I trotted away from the town. All the roads around here were dirt. Maybe there were some paved roads, but I sure didn't see any. I couldn't see anything at all through so many trees.

I bit my tongue to keep from speaking. There was so much to ask Mr. Rodney. And George wasn't saying a thing.

I couldn't stand it. So I faked a cough. A horse cough along with, "Mom and Dad."

"What was that?" Mr. Rodney said.

"Oh. Right, Gracie," George said. He cleared his throat. "Mr. Rodney, sir. We're looking for our Mom and Dad. We think they might be in your jail."

"I'm afraid not," Mr. Rodney said. "We have no women in the jail. Only two men, John Collingswood and George Barrett."

"That's a relief," I said. "Sort of." Then I sneezed. My huge horse nose was sucking up dust like a vacuum.

Mr. Rodney bent down and looked at my face. I pretended not to notice.

"Gracie and I—I mean *I* wonder if you have heard of Matthew and Laura Stockton?" George said. "I'm not sure when they were here. But maybe they were looking for school desks?"

"School desks?" said Mr. Rodney. "I don't know anything about those. But I do recall a woman named Laura Stockton."

Mom? I stumbled when Mr. Rodney said her name.

And George almost fell off my back.

"Whoa. Hold tight there, boy." Mr. Rodney said. Then he patted my neck.

"What about Laura Stockton?" George said.

"A wise woman, Mistress Stockton," said Mr.

Rodney. "She believes in freeing the colonies from British rule. She said a fight would be worth the hardships.

"That's our mom," I said. But I whinnied to cover it up.

"She traveled with a strange companion," Mr. Rodney said. "A bird. It rode on her shoulder. She called it Matthew. I found that odd."

A bird? Our dad was a bird? I let out a horse-y giggle. Which reminded me that I was a horse. And George wore tights. So it wasn't that funny after all. Well, maybe George in tights. And Dad as a bird. But not me being a horse.

"Is there something the matter with your horse?" Mr. Rodney said to George. "And is that a locket she's wearing? How unusual."

"Uh no," George said. Then he kicked me in the side. Which really, really hurt.

"That's her, uh, collar thing-y," he said.

I turned and glared at George and showed him my teeth. He moved his leg and mouthed "Sorry." Then he grinned. Like he was guilty. Which he was.

"Where is Laura Stockton now, sir?" George said. "When was the last time you saw her?" His voice got all squeaky and excited.

I held my breath. Not an easy trick when two people are riding on your back.

"I'm sorry. I don't know," Mr. Rodney said. "I haven't seen her in some time."

All of a sudden I missed my mom and dad a lot. A whole lot. I wanted to see them again. We *had* to find them.

"So she's not here," George said.

He sounded the way I felt. Sad.

We passed by a house here and there as we walked down the road. They weren't close together like the homes where we lived. Most were small and made of wood. Some were made of logs. Most weren't even painted. But most were surrounded by fields. One woman picked green onions from a garden near her front door.

"My house is the white one. Up ahead there," Mr. Rodney said.

I trotted him up close his front door. His big front door.

Mr. Rodney slid to the ground. "What is your name, boy?"

"I'm George Stockton." George patted my neck. "This is my sis—and this is Gracie."

"Go back to the tavern, George. The Golden Fleece on the Green. Many of the men in town meet there in the evening. Someone may be able to help you find your mother and her bird."

"We will," George said. "Thank you, Mr. Rodney."

Mr. Rodney walked up the stairs to his house like an old man. Real slow and careful. The door swung open. A woman in a long, light blue dress stepped out to help him.

But Mr. Rodney turned back to George and me.

"Be careful, George. This is a dangerous time in Dover," he said. "And good luck. I hope you find your mother and father."

Then he went inside.

"Do you know what a tavern is, George?" I said. I shimmied around some, wriggling my skin where Mr. Rodney had sat. "Because I don't."

"No," he said. "But we know the name of the place. Besides, this town isn't that big. We'll have to watch out for Crowe now, though."

I walked out of Mr. Rodney's front yard.

"George," I said. "I miss Mom and Dad. I hope we find them soon."

All we knew was that Mom wasn't a jailbird. And Dad was a bird bird.

George kicked me in the sides. "Get going," he said.

"Cut that out." I said. "You don't have to kick me. I know when to go."

"Well, that's the way the cowboys do it when they want their horse to move faster," he said. "So move faster."

"You asked for it," I said, and broke into a gallop.

George held onto to my mane for dear life. But he still slid from side to side.

"Just think," I said as I galloped along. "Mom might be at the tavern right now. With our father, the bird."

I couldn't give up on finding our parents. I wouldn't.

"I . . . hope . . . so," said George. He bounced all over the place on my back. He was a lousy rider. And a worse driver.

It took a while, but soon we came to the main street in town. I slowed down some in case there was a speed limit.

Up ahead to the left, I could see the steps where the people had thrown stones at Mr. Rodney. The stairs were empty now. The air was quiet.

A wooden sidewalk ran along the front of the buildings. The signs hanging outside told what kind of store each was.

One sign had a cup painted on it. On the cup was a picture of a snake twisted around a pole. Through the windows I could see shelves of bottles lining the walls.

Two women stood outside another store, talking. One held a basket. The other carried a bundle of fabric.

"There's The Golden Fleece Tavern," said George. He pointed to the sign. It showed a big horned sheep made of gold.

Out of nowhere, a man on a brown horse galloped across the grassy field. He headed right for us.

I had to turn away fast to get out of his way. "Hey . . . er . . . Neigh," I said. I bucked up on my back legs.

"Hey, Gracie. Whoa or something," said George. He slid right off my back. Then he landed on his bottom in the dirt.

"Are you okay, George?" I said. I turned to look down at him.

The man raced past us and stopped at The Golden Fleece Tavern. He jumped off his horse and ran inside.

"Are you trying to kill me?" George said. His tights had a rip in one knee. "Now see what you did."

"Sorry. But did you see that guy?" I whispered. My lips flapped. I couldn't help it. You try whispering with lips that big.

"You mean the one that tried to run over us?" George said. "No because . . . Hello? I was kind of busy. Falling on the ground."

He scowled at me.

"Get over it, George. That guy looks important. And important people know things," I said. "Maybe he knows where Mom and Dad are."

George stood up and brushed the dust off his pants. "Let's go," he said.

I knelt down so he could climb onto my back.

"No thanks," he said. "I'll walk."

"One little tumble," I said. I shook my head. "It was an accident, George. Honest."

"Yeah right," George said. He limped off.

We walked across the park to the tavern and stopped on the sidewalk.

"Go to that window," George said. He pointed. "And be ready."

"Ready for what?" I said.

"For a quick get-away," he said.

"What are you talking about?" I said. "A quick get-away from what?"

"Who knows," George said. "But I've got a funny feeling about this place. People are crazy here in Delaware. They throw rocks at you if you don't vote the way they do."

"True," I said. I waved a hoof goodbye.

George straightened his tights. Then he walked inside The Golden Fleece Tavern.

CHAPTER 7

I Spy

I think I just walked into a bar. And I'm only nine years old.

Plus, I'm wearing tights and short pants. Somebody would throw a rock at me for sure. Heck, I'd throw a rock at me if I had one.

The Golden Fleece Tavern was noisy and crowded. Men sat at tables drinking and talking and smoking pipes. Others ate food off dull silver plates. A man stood behind a long counter and poured drinks.

Now I knew for sure what a tavern was. It was a like a restaurant and a bar.

The room smelled like spoiled apple juice and bread and beef stew. And sweaty bodies and smoke. A tired looking lady in an apron hurried from table to table. She cleared dishes and brought food to waiting customers.

I glanced back at Gracie.

She watched me from outside the tavern. Her big black nose was pressed against the dirty window.

I walked by a wooden barrel. It smelled sour. What was in there?

I looked from side to side. No one noticed me. Not the man behind the counter, with the dirty apron and small wire frame glasses. Not the tired serving woman. No one seemed to care that a boy had walked into a tavern.

I reached inside the barrel.

"George?" Gracie called from outside.

I pretended like I couldn't hear her and fished around in the cool, stinky water. I pulled out a huge pickle.

"Put that back," Gracie said. Her voice was muffled and hoarse. Get it? *Horse*?

I turned around and waved with the pickle.

"Are you stealing that pickle?" Gracie said. She snorted at me. "Do you want to go to jail, with what's his name and what's his name?"

I waved her off. One little bite wouldn't hurt. I lifted the pickle to my mouth.

"Do you want to get stuck in time?" Gracie said. "Drop that pickle, George."

I stopped before I bit down. She was right. We couldn't take anything from the past. Or else we might get trapped here, too. Like Mom and Dad.

"Oh fine," I said. I dropped the pickle back into the barrel.

I wasn't liking this adventure so much. I had to wear goofy clothes. I had to ride a horse without a saddle. I was probably in danger. Plus I was starving.

I licked my fingers. *Mmmm.* Pretty good. And that bread and stew smelled yummy, too.

I walked toward the counter. I looked everywhere for Mom and Dad the bird. They weren't in the Golden Fleece Tavern.

That's when I saw him. He sat at a table near the back of the room.

A thin man with black hair and smoke gray eyes. Watching me.

Crowe!

"Psst."

I looked over my shoulder. Gracie stood behind me. Right inside the tavern.

She swished her tail. A table full of men stared at us. So did Crowe. But he didn't move. He just gave us a weird smile.

Lucky for me and Gracie, the tavern owner hadn't noticed a big black horse in his dining room. He was too busy serving drinks behind the counter.

"Gracie. I don't think horses are allowed in here," I whispered.

"See the guy leaning up against the counter. The one with the ponytail?" Gracie said. "He's the one that rushed in here."

"Don't look now," I said. "But Crowe is here too."

"Huh oh," Gracie said. Her ears perked up. "Where?"

"In the corner over there," I said. "Don't look at him."

Gracie looked.

"Erp," she said.

"Gosh, Gracie," I said. "I told you not to look. And then you did."

"Don't panic, George," Gracie said. She nudged me. "He doesn't recognize me. I mean, did I look like a horse when he saw us at the museum?"

I stared at her, blinking.

"Did I, George?"

"I'm thinking it over," I said.

She pawed my foot. "Ouch!" I said, real loud.

"Okay, you didn't look like a horse then," I said.

Gracie lifted her hoof. "Why does he keep raising his cup to me like that? And his eyebrows?"

"Because he saw us together when we gave Mr. Rodney a ride," I said. "He knows who you are, Gracie."

She looked at Crowe again.

"I don't like him at all," she said. She showed all her teeth at him.

The tired lady saw us. All of a sudden she didn't look tired anymore. She looked angry.

"Get that filthy beast out of my establishment," she said. She waved her apron at Gracie.

Gracie clomped toward the woman.

The woman held up her hands. "Here now," she said.

"I have secret business here, lady," Gracie said. "So butt out."

The woman dropped the cloth in her hand. She backed her way toward the stairs.

"Husband," she said. "I've worked too long. I'm

going up to bed." She took the stairs two at a time and disappeared.

The tavern was noisy and crowded. Which is why I guess the tavern owner still didn't see me or Gracie.

Gracie turned to me and grinned. Her yellow teeth stuck out.

"Those don't look so great," I said. "You need to floss."

The ponytail guy leaned across the counter toward the tavern owner. "I need to see Mr. Rodney," he said. His voice was low. "I have a message for him."

"Did you hear that?" I said to Gracie. "That guy knows Mr. Rodney."

I inched closer to the two of them so I could hear. So did Gracie.

The tavern owner went quiet. Several men standing at the counter did, too.

Something dangerous was about to happen. And Mr. Rodney was in the middle of it.

"What do you want with Mr. Rodney?" the tavern owner said.

"Go over and spy on them, George," Gracie said. She nudged me with her nose.

I stepped right up to the two men. The ponytail guy glanced at me. But he kept on talking.

Crowe watched us from his table. He sipped his drink from a big silver cup.

"I've come from Philadelphia," the ponytail guy said. "My errand is urgent. Haste is needed."

The tavern owner opened his mouth to answer.

Right then three British soldiers walked into the Golden Fleece Tavern.

They were dressed in red woolen jackets and white pants. They wore white wigs. Each man carried a long gun. They walked straight past Gracie.

Now *all* of the men in the room stopped talking and eating. Some glared at the soldiers. Some didn't look at them at all.

One of the soldiers stared at Gracie. "Why is there an animal in here?" he said.

"Wouldn't happen in England," another soldier said.

"Only in the Colonies. Americans are so uncivilized," the third said.

The soldiers walked to where I stood with the tavern owner and the ponytail guy.

The tallest one banged on the bar with his fist. My scalp prickled. These soldiers were big trouble.

"You there. Tavern Keeper. We've been told that rebels frequent this inn," the tall soldier said.

The guy with the ponytail moved close to me. He put his hand on my shoulder. I looked up at him. Then I glanced back at Crowe.

Crowe never took his eyes off me and Gracie.

"It's treason to speak against the Crown," said another soldier. He spoke to everyone in the bar.

"There are no rebels here," said the tavern owner. He looked worried. His eyes shifted to the guy with the ponytail.

"You there," said the first soldier. He motioned to the ponytail guy. "What is your business here?"

My heart pounded hard in my chest.

I saw Gracie gulp.

The guy with the ponytail bent. He looked me in the eyes. Then he straightened my jacket for me. And slipped something in my vest pocket.

"Go right home, son," he said.

"What?" I said.

"Make haste," the man said. "Tell your mother I may be late."

And then I knew. I had to go along with him. Mr. Rodney could be in danger if I didn't. Everyone at in the Golden Fleece Tavern could be in danger.

"Yes sir—I mean, yes, *Father*," I said. I turned around quick and started toward Gracie.

"The soldiers are watching you now," Gracie said. She didn't move her horse lips.

"Don't talk, Gracie," I whispered. "Did you notice they have g-u-n-s?"

A soldier raised his eyebrows.

Crowe gulped the last of his drink. He set his cup on the table with a thud and stood up.

"Down Gracie," I said.

Gracie knelt down so I could climb on her back. Right there in the middle of the tavern. Her feet made clomping sounds on the wooden floor as we backed out of the room.

Everyone watched. But nobody said a word. The door slammed shut behind us

The sun was going down. Soon it would be too dark for the soldiers or Crowe to see us.

Gracie stepped onto the dirt street.

I leaned on her neck. I couldn't breathe that great. I looked behind me as Gracie trotted away.

"Hurry, Gracie. Go faster," I said. "We have to get to —"

"Boy." It was one of the Redcoats from the tavern.

I almost wet my short pants.

Gracie was shaking so hard I almost slid off her back—again.

"Boy," the soldier said, louder. "Stop in the name of King George."

Me and Gracie froze.

CHAPTER 8

The British are Coming!

The British soldier looked angry. "Come over here, boy."

"Oh no," George said in my ear. "This is going to be much worse than somebody throwing rocks. It's going to be bullets this time."

"Want me to run?" I said. I trotted faster.

"Are you kidding?" George said. He pulled on my mane. "Don't you watch TV? Nobody shoots the horse. Just the rider. And that's me."

I stopped in the middle of the street. "Oh yeah? Then how come the horse is always falling down?" I said

I trotted toward the soldier as slow as I could. He must have been hot in all those clothes. His face was the same red color as his jacket.

"Yes sir?" George said.

"Didn't your parents teach you proper manners?" the soldier said. "Never bring a horse where people eat."

I nickered with happiness. No bullet for George. At least not yet.

"I'm sorry sir," George said. "My horse is stubborn and does as she pleases." He slapped my rump. "Bad, girl, Gracie. Bad."

I stopped nickering. That dumb George was a rat in tights.

"That's the spirit. Beat her and train her to do what is right," the soldier said. "If I ever see her in a tavern—or any building that is not a barn—I will beat her myself. And you, too. Do you understand me, boy?"

George nodded and mumbled another, "Yes sir."

The soldier marched back inside the tavern. But now Crowe stood in the doorway.

"Oh no," George said.

Crowe walked up to us. "George. Gracie," he said. "Here we are, together again."

"We gotta go," George said. He tugged on my mane.

"Wait. Listen to me," Crowe said. He took a step closer. "I can help you find your parents. But first you have to tell me where the time machine is."

"You don't want to help us," I said. I bared my teeth at him.

"You make a beautiful horse, Gracie," Crowe said. "The time machine can be tricky, can't it? Ask your grandfather. It turned him into a platypus once."

"Maybe we don't even know where the time machine is," George said.

Crowe spat on the ground. He smiled his slow smile. "Come now. Let's not play games. I can get your parents back. I'm the only person who can. Or didn't your grandfather tell you? I'm a time traveler, too."

I thought about seeing Mom and Dad again. A warm feeling filled my chest. I wanted to yell, "Let's make the deal. Quick." But George pulled at my mane. I knew he didn't want me to say another word.

"Show me," Crowe said, "where the time machine is. That's all you have to do." He petted my nose. "I'll get you back together with your parents. And as payment, maybe you can help me get home."

His voice sounded soft and even kind.

Maybe Crowe was telling the truth. Maybe Grandpa was wrong about him. "We left the time machine—"

George kicked me again. Harder.

"Yes?" Crowe said. He leaned toward me.

"Don't tell him anything, Gracie," George said. "Grandpa doesn't trust him. And neither do I."

I looked straight into Crowe's cold gray eyes. My horse sense told me that George was right.

I wasn't doing any more talking.

Crowe let out a long sigh.

"Have it your way," he said at last. "But I will always be close by. In case you change your mind. Remember that."

His voice didn't sound kind at all now.

I got the shivers.

"We won't change our minds," George said. "Ever." He nudged me with his knees.

George and I trotted away.

I could feel Crowe watching us.

For a long time, I was quiet.

Then I said, "Maybe Crowe can help us."

"I miss Mom and Dad, too, Gracie," George said. "But we can't give in to Crowe. They wouldn't want us to."

I squeezed my eyes shut for a moment. They stung from tears.

"Remember, Gracie," George said. "Mom and Dad warned us to stay away from that guy."

A big horse-y tear fell from my horse-y eye. It disappeared into the dusty road. But I don't think George saw.

We were both quiet. Then George said, "I almost forgot. The man with the ponytail gave me a letter or something. Go slow while I look at it."

"I'm not walking that fast, George," I said.

I heard crackling as George took the paper out of his pocket. "It's addressed to Mr. Caesar Rodney," he said. "That man wanted me to take this letter to him. I was afraid the soldier back there had seen it."

"I think we're safe now," I said. "As long as we can stay away from the British soldiers and Crowe." I let out a big breath. "So are we going to Mr. Rodney's house again?"

"Yes," George said.

I started off at a trot. George didn't even complain. We headed down the dirt road in the dark.

We hadn't gone along even for a minute before George bent low and grabbed tight to my mane.

"Quit pulling," I said.

"I hope you're a fast horse," George said. He sounded scared.

"I'm faster than you are," I said. "Even when I'm a girl. Why?"

"Because we're being followed."

I peered back over my shoulder past George's leg. Three riders were behind us. I could see their red uniforms.

Soldiers.

"Hold on tight, George," I said. "And I mean tight."

I ran off the road and into the woods. I raced through the trees. Bushes and limbs slapped at us.

"What the heck are you doing?" George yelled. "Are you trying to kill me?" He clung tight to my mane with both hands.

I couldn't believe how fast I could run. I made a terrific horse.

George had to duck to keep from getting knocked to the ground by low branches.

When we reached a thick grove of trees, I stopped. Mr. Rodney's house wasn't far now.

George rolled off my back.

"Hey, you're breathing hard," he said.

"That's what happens when you run, George," I said. "Next time how about if you run and I ride on your back?"

"Sure," said George. But he wasn't listening to me. He was too busy peering into the dark behind us.

We hid behind a stand of bushes and low trees. Then we waited for the riders to pass.

They never did.

"I think we lost them," George whispered.

My knees—or whatever they are on a horse—wobbled. "I hope so."

"Now I'm going to find out what's in this letter," George said.

"That's Mr. Rodney's," I said. "You could go to jail for opening someone else's mail."

"Not in 1776. Give me a break," George said. He pulled the letter out of his shirt. "We have to know what's going on." He put his finger on the wax seal to open it.

I snatched the letter out of his hands with my teeth.

"Hey!" George said.

"I shaid no, Georjch." Bleh. The letter tasted like George's sweat. "I'm going to find Misfter Rodney. Wif or wifout you. Good luck wif da British."

I galloped out of the grove. Up ahead was Mr. Rodney's home.

George chased after me. "Gracie, you sure can get on your high horse," he said. "Get it? High horse?"

"Hush Georjch," I said. "The woodsch are full of enemiesch."

George caught up with me at Mr. Rodney's front steps.

"Wait," George said. Now he was breathing hard. "A horse can't hand Mr. Rodney a secret message."

"Yesch, I can."

George reached for the letter. I moved away and he almost grabbed my locket.

"Watch it," I said. "I'm bigger than you are now."

"Sorry," said George. "I won't open the letter."

"Promish?" I said.

"I promish. I mean, promise," George said.

I let George have the letter. It had teeth marks and horse slobber on it.

"Gross," George said. He wiped his hands on his short brown pants.

"Serves you right," I said. I nudged George a lit-

tle. "Be serious now. Get up to the door and give that letter to Mr. Rodney."

I followed close behind and pushed him along.

George lifted the doorknocker. He let it fall three times. Then he waited.

The door opened.

A girl answered. "May I help you?"

She peered around George to me.

I grinned at her.

"Oh," she said. She took a step backward.

"Here," George said. He held out the letter. "This is for Mr. Rodney."

"Mr. Rodney is not taking callers tonight. He is ill."

"Okay. Thanks anyway," George said. He turned to leave. But I wouldn't let him past.

"Go on, George," I said between my teeth.

The woman looked at me in surprise.

"Did your horse say something?" she said. She backed up again.

"Actually, this is my twin sister." George smiled.

It's official. George is a dumb dumb head.

The girl looked from me to George and back again. She started to close the door.

"Wait. It's important," George said.

A voice from inside the house called out, "Who is it, Elizabeth?"

The girl answered. "A horse and her boy, Mr. Rodney. I mean, a boy and his horse."

I gave a horse laugh. George elbowed me a good one.

"They have a message for you," said Elizabeth.

"From a man at The Golden Fleece Tavern," George called into the house.

Mr. Rodney appeared in the doorway. He didn't have his green scarf on this time. His face was scarred something awful.

I gasped. George stepped back into me. He pushed on his glasses.

When Mr. Rodney saw us he pulled his scarf over his face. Only his eyes showed. He leaned against the door like he was too tired to stand.

"I'm sorry if I scared you," he said. "My poor pocked face has that effect, I'm afraid. Did you find your mother?" He sounded even weaker than he had this morning.

"No sir. But we've brought you a message," George said. "It's from some guy at the Golden Fleece."

He handed the letter to Mr. Rodney.

Mr. Rodney looked at the seal. "It's from Thomas McKean in Philadelphia."

"Come in, boy," said Mr. Rodney.

"Can my sister come in, too?" George said.

For once George was smart.

"Of course," Mr. Rodney said.

I held my horse head high. And clomped into the house behind George.

CHAPTER 9

Mr. Rodney Spills the Beans

Elizabeth had to open the door wide for Gracie to get through.

"Thank you," Gracie said.

"Shh, Gracie," I said. "You're going to freak people out."

And I was right. Elizabeth looked as if she might faint dead away.

I glanced around the room. All the furniture and stuff looked brand new. No wonder Mom and Dad had wanted to bring stuff back from the past.

"Here, here now," said Mr. Rodney when he saw Gracie in his living room. He put his hands up to stop her.

"I said the boy's sister could come in. Not his horse, Elizabeth, " said Mr. Rodney. "Have the boy's horse taken to the stables. Be sure Jeremy brushes her down. Have him give her water and oats as well."

"Um, Mr. Rodney," I said. "That's no horse. That's my sister."

"That's right," Gracie said. "I look like a horse on the outside. But on the inside, I am a lot like a girl."

Elizabeth edged away from us. "Merciful heaven," she said.

Mr. Rodney looked from Gracie to me, then to the note.

"I know she's funny looking," I said. "Even when Gracie is normal, people think she's strange."

"Hey," Gracie said.

She showed me all her teeth.

And I got behind Mr. Rodney.

"Did I hear your horse speak again?" Mr. Rodney said. "I must be sicker than I thought. Perhaps I should return to my bed."

Instead he eased himself down on a big velvet

couch nearby.

I sat next to him. "I told you. Gracie's my sister," I said. "She just looks like a horse."

"I see," he said. He kept his eyes on Gracie. And on me.

Gracie sat next to me. "Scoot over, George," she said. "I'm squished."

I moved over.

So did Mr. Rodney.

I looked for Elizabeth. She must have backed all the way out of the room.

"You can't go to bed now, Mr. Rodney," I said. "This message is important."

"We've come a long way to bring it to you," Gracie said. "A real long way."

"I thought you were lost," Mr. Rodney said. He rubbed at his eyes.

"Our parents are lost," I said. "And we're looking for them. It's a kind of a long story."

"I'll neigh," Gracie said. "I mean, I'll say."

Mr. Rodney blinked. Gracie smiled.

"Think of me as a girl in a horse costume," she said. "That's what George thought at first."

Mr. Rodney blinked again. And again. He was doing a lot of blinking.

"Something weird is going on around here, Mr. Rodney," I said. "That man in the tavern said he was looking for you. And then right away the British soldiers came in like they knew about your letter."

"And then they chased us," Gracie said.

I frowned at her. "You're sliding off the seat," I said.

"Oh," she said. She scooted back and crossed her legs.

Talk about weird.

Mr. Rodney opened the letter and read it. "This looks like trouble," he said. "Thomas says the Delaware vote for independence is tied."

He stood. "I must get to Philadelphia now and break the tie. It's important that Delaware stand together with the other colonies. We must all be united if we are to win our freedom from England."

Mr. Rodney put the letter on a small roll top desk.

"What's going on, Mr. Rodney?" Gracie said.

Mr. Rodney stared at Gracie. He looked like he still wasn't quite used to a talking horse.

I wasn't used to that either.

"The Colonies are casting votes," Mr. Rodney said. "Votes for freedom from British rule."

"Won't that make the British mad?" I said.

Mr. Rodney nodded. "They call it treason. And it is against the law. Not everyone wants to break away from England. But many of us feel we must be free to rule ourselves."

"So why do you have to go to Philadelphia?" Gracie said.

Mr. Rodney leaned on a large round table. He touched his green scarf and took a deep breath.

"Most of the delegates from the thirteen colonies are in Philadelphia right now. Me and George Read and Thomas McKean represent Delaware. But I became ill and had to return to Dover. In my absence, George Read has voted against independence. And Thomas has voted *for* independence. So they are tied. And I must get to Philadelphia in time to break the tie."

Mr. Rodney pounded the table with his fist. "Delaware will not vote for independence unless I am there to break the tie," he said. "And unless we are united, the Colonies' fight for freedom may fail before it even begins."

CHAPTER 10

Gracie Stockton, Freedom Rider

Elizabeth must have heard Mr. Rodney pounding the table.

She came to the door. Her eyes went wide when she saw me sitting on the couch. And she kept her distance.

"I must leave for Philadelphia without delay," Mr. Rodney said. "Please inform Cook that I will need something to eat for the trip."

"But Mr. Rodney," Elizabeth said. She looked worried. "You're too sick. You mustn't go."

"It cannot be helped," Mr. Rodney said.

"As you wish, Mr. Rodney." Elizabeth left again.

"I could go for a little something to eat myself," said George. "The last thing I almost ate was a pickle."

"You big baby," I said. I noticed Mr. Rodney looking at me funny. He came close and opened my mouth.

"Hey," I said. "What are you . . . ?"

Before I could finish, he let my lips flap shut. Then he ran his hands down my horse legs.

"That tickles," I said, letting out a horse-y giggle.

Mr. Rodney turned back to George. "She seems fit," he said. "Except that she talks. Quite a bit."

"Not a bit of fat on me," I said.

Elizabeth came back in the room. "Cook is preparing for the trip, Mr. Rodney."

"Excellent," he said. Then he looked at me. "She'll do, if you'll allow it, George."

"Do?" I said.

"Do what?" George said.

"For the long journey to Philadelphia, of course," said Mr. Rodney. "Take her to the barn and have her saddled, Elizabeth. Make haste. What we do now may decide the fate of our thirteen colonies."

"Wait a minute," George said. "You mean . . . "

"I get to go to Philadelphia, too?" I said. Now *this* was exciting. "We get to travel together? Wow. I'll find the barn on my own. Thanks anyway, Elizabeth."

Elizabeth nodded. "Very well, Gracie," she said. She smiled at me. But she still didn't get too close.

"I'll ride you to Philadelphia if your owner agrees," Mr. Rodney said. He shook his head. "I cannot believe I am talking to a horse."

"Uh . . . he's my brother," I said. "Not my owner." I snorted.

"Sure, Mr. Rodney. Get going, Gracie." George slapped my rump.

"Watch it," I said.

I had to do a lot of stepping back and forth in the front room. But soon I was out the door and headed to the barn. There I stood as still as I could. Jeremy, the stable boy, fastened belts and buckles around me. The saddle was on. It itched. And it was hot.

"Open up, girl," Jeremy said. Then he tried to put a bit in my mouth.

"No thanks," I said. I turned my head away. "Just a harness, please."

Jeremy's eyes widened. You'd think people could

get over the talking horse thing.

"You . . . *talk*?" he said.

"And I bite," I said. I showed my teeth to Jeremy. "So don't you try putting that thing in my mouth. I have no idea where it's been."

In a few minutes I was ready to go. Itchy back and all. Jeremy didn't look too great, though.

Mr. Rodney met me out in the barn.

"We have eighty miles to ride," he said. "And we must travel fast. We need to be in Philadelphia before the last man votes. Can you get me there in time, Gracie?"

"I can, Mr. Rodney," I said. But I crossed my hooves. For luck.

∞∞

If anyone tells you that riding eighty miles is easy, don't believe them.

Especially if you are the horse.

It was a long, hard ride.

And sweaty.

And I got bit by flies the whole way.

And did I say long?

Mr. Rodney had a hard time staying on my back. He coughed a lot, and leaned on my neck most of the time. He was really sick.

All day Mr. Rodney and I ran.

The sun beat down on us.

And that night, it rained. Lightning lit the sky. Trees waved in the storm. The raindrops stung.

"We must keep going, Gracie," Mr. Rodney said. "Be strong."

We had stopped to rest. The rain pounded us. Mr. Rodney coughed. His voice sounded weak.

"I am doing my best," I said.

"That's a good horse," Mr. Rodney said. He patted my neck. "Er, I mean girl."

He gave me a carrot. And then we were off again.

I ran and ran over the rough roads.

Through mud.

In the dark.

Mr. Rodney coughed most of the night.

But we made it. We rode into Philadelphia the next day.

My legs shook. I had a hard time breathing. I could feel sweat dripping off my sides.

People on the streets watched us as we hurried into town. I almost ran into a few of them. I couldn't believe we made it the whole eighty miles.

"This is the Pennsylvania State House, Gracie,"

said Mr. Rodney, when we stopped in front of a big red building. He jumped to the ground. He stumbled. I caught his shirt in my teeth and held him steady.

"Thank you, Gracie," he said. He patted my neck again.

I nodded to him.

He walked up the steps.

For a moment I thought he was going to fall. But he didn't.

Mr. Rodney strode into the building. I followed close behind. He walked into a room full of men. I watched from the doorway.

"He's here," I heard someone say.

"We didn't know if you would make it," said another man.

"Will you cast your vote for Delaware, Mr. Rodney?" a man said. He wore a powdered wig.

"I will," Mr. Rodney said.

He was splattered with mud. His hair was a mess. His green scarf was filthy. But he looked great to me.

Mr. Rodney stood at the front of the room. "I vote for independence," he said.

A cheer went up in the room. I let out a whinny.

"Freedom! Freedom!" the men said.

Everyone clapped and yelled. I stomped the floor with my hooves.

And I called out, too. "Freedom!"

CHAPTER 11

A Long Wait

I waited for Gracie at Mr. Rodney's house for three whole days.

I was worried. What if the British soldiers had captured Gracie and Mr. Rodney? And put them in jail?

We would never get home.

And we would be stuck in 1776 forever.

While I waited, Elizabeth made me fix stuff around the farm. I guess I'm handy like Grandpa. Who knew?

The first day I nailed loose boards on the side of the barn.

The next day I watered the garden corn using a heavy bucket. I had to fill the bucket from the well.

On the third day, Elizabeth said, "Would you chop the long grass in front of the house?"

I said, "Sure. Where's the lawn mower?"

She frowned. Then she handed me a long curved blade on a short stick.

"Hey," I said. "Isn't this what that guy, Death, carries around?"

Elizabeth rolled her eyes. "It's called a sycthe," she said. Then she walked away. Fast.

All this fixing and stuff made me miss Grandpa. And the Stockton Museum of Just About Everything in American History.

And even Gracie.

On the fourth morning, I stacked stones in the yard to make a wall. I rubbed my blistered hands together.

"Don't you ever do anything fun around here?" I said to Elizabeth.

But she wasn't listening. She was looking off down the road.

"Someone's coming this way," she said. She shaded her eyes with her hand.

I squinted and looked up the road. My stomach

did a flip flop.

"Oh my gosh. Two British soldiers," I said. "Hide me, Elizabeth."

"This way." Elizabeth ran to the barn. I was so scared my legs wouldn't move. But I followed her anyway.

Jeremy was there. He was polishing a saddle.

"Jeremy, hide George," Elizabeth said. She was out of breath. "The soldiers are here."

"Hiding in here won't do," Jeremy said. "They will find you. You gotta run."

He pulled a loose board off the back wall of the barn.

"Hey," I said. "I just hammered all those in place."

"Be quick," he said.

"I'm not nailing that board back," I said.

"Hurry, George," Jeremy said. He pulled at my shirt. "Get going."

I climbed through the hole. "Keep those soldiers busy, please," I said to Elizabeth and Jeremy.

Jeremy opened his eyes wide. "Busy?" he said. "How?"

One of the soldiers appeared in the barn door.

I ducked out of sight.

"You there," I heard the soldier say to Jeremy. "Where's your master?"

"What did you say?" said Jeremy. "My sister? She's in Dover. She has a job in town."

He was doing a good job of stalling.

I climbed through the hole. And Elizabeth stuck the board back in place before the soldier saw me.

I ran toward the trees beyond the barn. I was so scared, even my hair was shaking.

"There he is," shouted the other soldier.

Drat. I forgot about the other soldier. He must have been waiting outside the barn.

I looked back over my shoulder as I ran. Both soldiers chased me. Then one of them stopped. He knelt and pointed his rifle at me.

"Stop, boy," the soldier yelled.

"Leave the child alone," Elizabeth said.

I ran as fast as I could. I heard the sound of a gunshot. A bullet whizzed past my ear.

My stomach froze up like a chunk of ice. I was going to die. And I was going to die wearing tights.

Now Elizabeth's voice was a scream. "Run, George."

Through the trees I ran. One soldier chased after me. The one with the rifle. I didn't know where the other guy went.

I tripped and almost fell over a dead branch.

"Help," I said. "Grandpa? Gracie? Anybody?"

But Grandpa couldn't hear me. And Gracie was in Pennsylvania starting a war. If she even got to Pennsylvania.

Bang! Another shot.

Too close. Sheesh.

"Hey," I yelled. "I'm only nine years old."

I zigged and zagged as I ran.

My lungs were about to pop.

I was running far from Mr. Rodney's house. Would Gracie be able to find me when she got back?

Would I live to see her get back?

This was not good. I did not want to die in 1776. It would mess up my whole life.

I ran out of the trees and into a field of corn to hide. I couldn't see the soldiers anymore. I stopped to rest.

Then I heard the sound of horses' hooves behind me. They were galloping fast. So *that's* why I didn't see those soldiers. They'd gone back for their horses.

"He's gone into the corn," a voice said.

I should have stayed hidden. But I panicked. I bolted through the cornfield.

The pounding hooves were almost on top of me.

I ran faster. But my legs were so weak. I knew I couldn't outrun those horses.

Ka-Blam! A bullet zipped through the tops of the corn near my head.

"Goodbye, Gracie," I said. "Goodbye, Grandpa. Goodbye, world."

Something hit me from behind. I fell flat on my face.

I'd been shot. But it didn't even hurt. I felt around for blood.

"What do you mean, goodbye? I just got here, George."

"Gracie?" I lifted my head.

Gracie stared down at me. She wore a dirty green scarf around her neck. It covered her locket.

She snipped off an ear of corn with her teeth. "Yesh, of courshe it'sh me. And I'm shtarving."

She swallowed and burped. "Oh. I think I just threw up a little."

"Gracie," I said. "You're stealing corn. You're gonna get us trapped in Delaware."

"I'm not stealing, George," Gracie said. "Mr. Rodney said I could have as much corn as I wanted."

Another bullet shot through the stalks. Gracie ducked.

"We've got to get out of here, George," she said. "Climb up. We're going home."

I scrambled onto Gracie's back and we raced away.

Out of the cornfield.

Ahead of the soldiers' guns.

Away down the dirt road.

Past farms and clumps of trees and pastures of cows.

Toward Dover and the time machine.

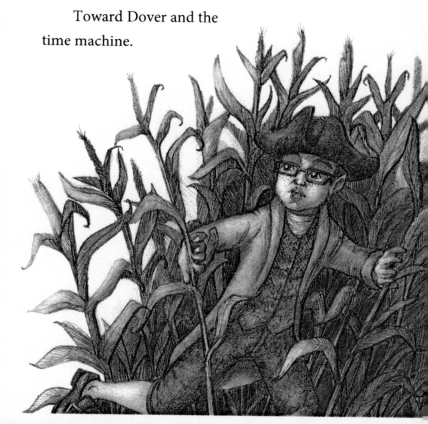

CHAPTER 12

Only a Glimpse

Soon the soldiers were way behind me and George. Now they were two blurry spots on the road.

"Can you believe how fast I am, George?" I yelled out to him. The wind blew my mane back as I flew down the road. "You should have seen me on the road to Philadelphia. I'm faster than a speeding bullet, as you can see."

"Great," George yelled back. He leaned down close to my ear. "Gracie. I'm happy to see you and all. But from up here, well, you're all slimy. And you stink. Bad."

"You're welcome for saving your life," I said.

George is so ungrateful. "Sheesh. It's not like I had time to shower. I've been sort of busy starting the American Revolution."

"Oh, yeah, sorry. Thanks for the help," George said. "How'd the ride with Mr. Rodney go?"

"Pretty good," I said. "Mr. Rodney was sick the whole way. But we made it. And look at this." I lifted my head so George could see. "He gave me this green scarf for helping him."

George touched the silky material. "Cool," he said. "It sure is dirty, though."

I told you George is ungrateful.

I slowed down when we could see Dover up ahead.

The street was almost empty. Some women in long dresses carried baskets of bread and vegetables. A couple of men stood outside a store talking. A little boy ran past us. He was chasing a metal ring the size of a wagon wheel. He hit it with a stick to keep it rolling ahead of him.

"There's the school," I said. I slowed to a walk. "Try to act normal, George. We don't want to attract attention."

"The talking horse says that to me?" George said.

I kept checking over my shoulder for the soldiers. They couldn't have given up so soon.

"What do we do now?" I said. "I mean, how are we supposed to get home? Does the time machine come and pick us up or what?"

"First of all, we keep an eye out for Crowe," George said. "And the guys with guns."

"And then what?" I said.

"How should I know?" George said. "I guess we climb into the outhouse and it will take us back. Like magic."

"What about Mom and Dad, George?" I said. "Do we just leave them here? I don't want to do that." I was so tired from running. And getting shot at. And worrying about our parents.

"Gracie, you know they can't come with us. We still have lots of stuff still at the museum. They can't come home until we take it all back, remember? Every bit."

It wasn't fair. But George was right. I wasn't even sure if *we* would be able to get home.

We trotted past the school. I peered in the windows. I saw six kids. All boys. They wrote with feather pens on small boards they held on their laps. The teacher talked to them from the front of the room. A little boy looked out the window at us and grinned. When I grinned back, his mouth fell open.

I stopped when we got to the outhouse. I hoped it was the right one. The outhouse that was also a time machine.

"Okay, George," I said. "Now what?" I kept my voice low as I glanced around. I still hoped Mom and Dad would show up. But not the soldiers.

George slid off my back. "We get in the time machine, I guess," he said.

"Okay," I said. "You first. I'll follow."

"How are we both going to fit in *there*?" he said. He pointed at the narrow wooden building. "You're a pretty fat horse, don't forget."

"I am not fat," I said. "I'm big boned. And I don't know how we're both going to fit either. Maybe I'll get a run at it and jump in."

George backed up a step.

"Not with me in there. You first," he said.

I guess he didn't want to be smashed dead like a fly. Not in an outhouse.

"I think I have an idea," George said.

That's when I heard a big bunch of noise.

George ran to the corner of the house. I followed and peeked over his shoulder.

The two soldiers from Mr. Rodney's house were

on the green. And a lot of people and some more soldiers were talking to them. Soldiers with guns.

I hunched down low. "George," I said.

"Be quiet, Gracie," George said. "I'm thinking, I'm thinking."

One of the soldiers saw me and pointed.

"Uh, George . . . " I said.

"I've got it. I'll ride you into the outhouse," George said.

"Great," I said. "How about right now?"

The soldiers raced toward us. I bent low and George scrambled up on my back.

"Go, Gracie, go," he said.

"Hold on, George." I backed up a few steps. Then I galloped toward the outhouse.

When I hit the door, I got stuck. George fell over my head. And landed in the outhouse. Most of me was in, too, but my rump still stuck out.

Very unladylike.

The soldiers shouted. They were coming closer.

George stood up. My nose was in his face.

"We're dead," he said, into my left nostril.

"Don't be so negative, George," I said. "We're not dead yet. Help me. Quick."

He put his feet on my shoulders and pushed

hard. I came loose with a big *pop*! Like a giant cork bursting out of a bottle. I stumbled backwards.

A bullet hit the outhouse.

"Hurry, Gracie," George said.

"Protect your face," I said.

I charged at the outhouse door again.

George scrunched into a corner and hid his eyes with both arms.

With a *BAM*! I was in. Standing on my back hooves. George stood behind me. He was smashed up against the outhouse wall. And my tail was in his face.

The outhouse lit up like a spaceship. It shuddered.

"It worked," George yelled.

"Hold on, I said. "This thing's going to take off any second."

Someone hollered, "They're in the outhouse."

"We're moving," I said. I gulped, thinking about leaving Mom and Dad behind.

"Wait," George said. "Gracie, where's Mr. Rodney's green scarf?"

"On my neck," I said. I touched it with my hoof. "But Mr. Rodney gave it to me. For bravery."

"We can't take anything back with us, remember?" he said.

He was right. Again. But I didn't want him to be.

"Oh, right. Pull it off, George. Quick."

The outhouse began to spin.

George climbed over my rump and onto my back. I felt a big punch in the stomach.

"Watch it, would you?" I said.

George felt around for the scarf. "I got it," he said. He pulled it off and threw it out the door.

I waved as it flew away on the wind.

We were spinning now. Slow, like when a merry-go-round first gets going.

As we turned, I caught glimpses of the soldiers standing outside. A couple scratched their heads. I guess they'd never seen a boy on a horse spinning around and around in an outhouse before.

A woman ran toward us with a bird on her shoulder. My heart jumped in my chest.

"George, look," I said. "That's Mom . . . and Dad, the bird."

"I see them," George said.

"Mom," he called. "Dad." He waved his arms.

Mom waved back at us. She said something. But I couldn't hear her.

"Mom," I said. But the word came out a neigh.

"Dad."

I felt sick from spinning around and around.

The outhouse spun faster.

"Wait," I said. I kicked at the walls. "We have to stop this thing. We have to take Mom and Dad with us."

But the outhouse spun and rose off the ground. A huge burst of air blew the soldiers' hats off. I saw a man faint.

Now I could only see tiny glimpses of Mom and the bird. We were spinning too fast.

"Be . . . careful," Mom shouted.

The bird squawked. "Crowe."

"Mom, jump on," George shouted back. "You can do it." He hung out the door and held his hand out to her.

She shook her head. "Watch out," she said again. She looked so worried. She pointed. Then she and the bird—I mean Dad faded out of sight.

"Mom. Dad," I called.

But they were gone.

Crowe pushed through the crowd. He raced toward us.

Too late I screamed at George to get back inside.

Crowe jumped at the spinning outhouse and

grabbed George by the leg.

"Help me, Gracie," he said.

I bit onto the back of George's pants and pulled.

Crowe held on to George's shoe.

"Let me in that time machine," Crowe said. He tried to climb up George.

"Kick, George," I said.

George tried to kick Crowe off. "Let go of my shoe," he said.

"Let me in that blasted machine," Crowe said. "Or no one goes home."

I could feel my front hooves slipping out the door.

"I can't hold on, George," I said.

Then George turned crazy wild.

He kicked and kicked and kicked.

Crowe shrieked and let go.

Then he disappeared.

And George and me? We fell backward into the outhouse.

I mean, the time machine.

And *zoom*, we were in the black hole.

CHAPTER 13

There's No Place Like Home

The time machine landed with a *thud*. Gracie and I tumbled out. Right on top of Grandpa.

The time machine burped.

"George! Gracie!" Grandpa said, from happiness this time. I could see it in his face. He was glad we were back.

"Grandpa," Gracie said. "I'm so glad to see you." She squeezed him around the neck.

Grandpa laughed and hugged us both.

"We're home," I said.

Then Gracie pulled away from Grandpa's hug. "We saw Mom and Dad." Her bottom lip quivered. "But they wouldn't come with us."

"We left them behind, Grandpa," I said. "We left Mom and Dad in Dover in the middle of a war. And Crowe is there with them."

"And Dad's a bird," Gracie said.

"A bird?" Grandpa said. He frowned and thought for a second. "Once I was a platypus in the St. Louis zoo. I craved fish for weeks after that."

"Yeah, Crowe told us about that," I said.

Grandpa raised his eyebrows. "Crowe? He found you?"

Gracie nodded. Her eyes filled with tears. I felt like crying, too.

"We should have saved Mom and Dad," I said.

"But you knew your parents couldn't come with you," said Grandpa. "Not until you return every single thing they took from the past. And we're only guessing that will bring them home."

"Yeah, we figured." My whole body slumped. A bunch of stuff from the past. A bunch of ding dang stuff from fifty states. That was going to be hard.

Gracie sniffed and touched her locket.

Then I noticed something.

"Hey Gracie," I said. "You're not a horse anymore."

Gracie sniffed again. She looked down at herself. Then at me.

"You're not wearing tights anymore," she said.

"That's a relief," I said. I pulled one pant leg up. I had a big scratch on my ankle. "That must be where Crowe grabbed me."

"Crowe got that close to you?" Grandpa said.

I could tell by his face that he was worried. And angry.

"Don't worry, Grandpa," she said. "George can kick harder than a horse."

I laughed and punched Gracie in the arm.

Then she punched me. Even harder.

"Ouch," I said.

Everything was back to normal.

Almost.

"I am glad you're both home safe," said Grandpa. He pulled us close. "I was worried about you two. Even though you were gone for just a few seconds."

"What?" I said.

"Grandpa," Gracie said. "We were gone for days."

Grandpa shook his head. "To you it was days. But to me it was a few seconds. That's the magic of the time travel."

The time machine let out a little sigh. All of its lights went dark. Like it was asleep.

But it wasn't a stinky outhouse anymore. It had turned into an old trunk.

taptaptap Tap—Tap—Tap taptaptap

The three of us looked at each other.

The telegraph machine. Again.

taptaptap Tap—Tap—Tap taptaptap

"Could it be . . . ?" Grandpa said.

"Mom and Dad," Gracie and I said together.

We all ran to the telegraph.

Grandpa grabbed a pad and pencil and wrote the words.

"George . . . and Gracie . . . okay?"

The telegraph went quiet.

"Your parents are worried about you." Grandpa sent a message back. "Kids . . . are . . . fine. . . . Where . . . are . . . you?"

Gracie touched her locket. "George," she whispered. "They need our help."

"I know, Gracie," I said.

We had to take another ride in the time machine. We had to rescue Mom and Dad.

And we knew Crowe would be there, too. Waiting for us. Wherever we ended up.

"Where are they now, Grandpa?" I said.

"I don't know, kids," Grandpa said. "I can't get an answer." He wiggled the telegraph and looked all around it. "This thing isn't working anymore."

Something caught my eye. A red light. Blinking on the big map next to Grandpa's desk.

"Look," I said, pointing.

"Mom and Dad are telling us where they are," Gracie said.

"We're the only ones who can bring them home," I said. I put my hand on Gracie's shoulder. "We have to go."

Gracie touched her necklace. She nodded.

"I don't like it," Grandpa said. "Crowe will be

there wherever you land. Waiting."

"But we have to do it," Gracie said. "You know it, too, Grandpa."

Grandpa stared at the light. It blinked.

And blinked.

And blinked some more.

Then he looked at me and Gracie. He touched our cheeks.

Then he nodded. "It's time," he said.

We all walked to the map.

THE END . . . OR IS IT?

GEORGE & GRACIE TELL THE REAL STORY OF...

Caesar Rodney

Hi. This is Gracie.

And this is George. We're going to tell you the true story of Caesar Rodney. Gracie's going to start. Right Gracie?

Right, George. Here goes. Caesar Rodney was born in Dover, Delaware in 1728. His father was a farmer. Caesar had a happy life as a kid. But his father died when Caesar was 17 years old, which was probably hard for him.

Wow. I didn't know that, Gracie.

Isn't that sad, George? Anyway, when Caesar grew up he had a lot of different jobs. For most of his jobs, he had something to do with making laws for the people in Delaware. When he got older, he became a member of the first American congress. It was called the Continental Congress.

When did he sign the Declaration of Independence, Gracie? I mean, didn't the guys in Congress write it?

Yes, George. But you're telling my part now.

Oh. Sorry, Gracie.

That's okay, George. Anyway, England made the people in America pay taxes. The Americans didn't get to vote yes or no for these taxes, which made a lot of people mad. Many Americans wanted to be free from England. But Caesar and the other men in Congress gave everyone a chance to vote for independence. They made the rule that all thirteen states in America would have to vote yes if they wanted to be free from England.

This is my part, isn't it Gracie?

Not quite, George. Caesar Rodney and two other delegates from Delaware, Thomas McKean and George Read, were sent to Philadelphia, Pennsylvania in June to vote for the state of Delaware. Now it's your turn, George.

Thanks, Gracie. Okay, here's where the story gets good.

That's a nice thing to say, George.

Sorry. Where was I? Oh, yeah. Not all the representatives from the thirteen colonies would agree to declare independence. Not everyone wanted to be free from England. So the Continental Congress took a break for a few weeks. They called it a recess. But I don't think they got to play on the playground during their recess.

George . . . stick to the story.

Don't be so bossy, Gracie. Anyway, Caesar had to go home to Dover before the Congress met again for the final vote. While Caesar was gone, the other two Delaware delegates had a problem. George Read decided to vote *against* independence. But Thomas McKean wanted to vote yes. And they needed Caesar to break the tie. So Thomas McKean sent an urgent letter to Caesar by special messenger asking him to return to Philadelphia and vote.

That's the part in our story where me and George see the ponytail guy with the letter. He was the special messenger, remember George?

Yeah, that's right, Gracie. Now can I finish my part?

Who's stopping you?

Okay. The thing is that Caesar didn't get the message until the day before the vote. He had to really hurry to get to Philadelphia in time. He rode eighty miles on horseback when he was very, very sick.

George, tell them what kind of sickness he had.

I was going to, Gracie. He had asthma all his life, but he also had skin cancer on his face. So he was pretty sick. But he traveled all night through a thunderstorm anyway. He wanted Delaware to vote for independence. He got to Independence Hall in Philadelphia on July 2, 1776 a couple of minutes before the delegates voted, and he voted yes. He and the other delegates signed the Declaration of Independence on July 4, 1776.

One more important thing to tell them, George, is that we celebrate the 4th of July every year to remember the day the Declaration of Independence was signed.

I know that, Gracie. Gosh.

Well, George. I bet you didn't know that Caesar Rodney actually gave his life for his country. Did you?

I . . . huh . . . okay, no I didn't, Gracie.

Well, he did George. Remember the skin cancer? Well, it made ugly sores and scars on Caesar's face. He became so deformed that he never appeared in public without a green scarf to hide his face.

Oh yeah, Gracie. That's why he's wearing it in our story.

Yes, that's because his face looked so bad. But here's the other part of that story. In Caesar Rodney's lifetime, the only place to be cured of skin cancer was in England. After Caesar signed the Declaration of Independence, he could not go back to England. If he did, he would be arrested and hanged for treason. Caesar knew that he might die if he signed the Declaration, but he signed it anyway. He believed in freedom for America. In 1784, Caesar Rodney did finally die of skin cancer.

Is that the end, Gracie?

Yes. That's the whole story. Say goodbye now, George.

Goodbye now, George.

Very funny, George.

Delaware State Facts

- **Statehood:** December 7, 1787, the first state to ratify the Constitution of the United States
- **Origin of Name:** Named for Sir Thomas West, Lord De La Warr, Governor of Virginia in 1610
- **State Capital:** Dover, capital since 1777
- **State Flag:** Colonial blue background, coat of arms inside a buff-colored diamond, date of statehood below the diamond. The coat of arms: farmer and a rifleman on either side of a shield. The state motto is on a banner below the shield.
- **Nicknames:** First State, Diamond State, Blue Hen State
- **Song:** Our Delaware
- **Motto:** Liberty and Independence
- **Flower:** peach blossom
- **Tree:** American holly
- **Bird:** blue hen chicken
- **Insect:** Ladybug
- **Colors:** Colonial blue and buff

Delaware Curiosities

- Pirates used to attack the shores of Delaware Bay off and on from 1609 to 1788.

- Old Swedes Church in Wilmington, Delaware is the oldest church still being used in the United States and was dedicated on July 4, 1699.

- Blackbeard the pirate buried stolen treasure in a hideaway at Blackbird Creek on the coast of Delaware around 1717 and 1718. The treasure has never been found.

- Legend has it that Betsy Ross's flag was first held up in battle at Cooch's Bridge near Newark, Delaware on September 8, 1777.

- The Methodist Church of America was organized in 1784 at Barratt's Chapel in Frederica, Delaware.

- The Governor's house in Dover, Delaware was once a stop on the Underground Railroad from about 1825 to 1865.

- Nylon was first created and produced in Seaford, Delaware in 1934 and 1935.

- You can see the largest cargo plane in the western world, the C-5 Galaxy, at Dover Air Force Base.

- The Heimlich Maneuver (a way to stop someone from choking) was invented Dr. Henry Heimlich in 1974. Dr. Heimlich was born in Wilmington, Delaware on February 3, 1920.

- Delaware is the second smallest state by land size in the United States.

Get a sneak peak of what happens next!

CHAPTER 1

Off and Runny

"Aa-chew," said Gracie. "Excuse me."

I took off my glasses and wiped them on my shirt. "Could you aim that spit at somebody else, please?"

"Can I help it if I'm allergic to you, George?" Gracie said. She smiled at me.

A huge map of the United States is pinned on the fix-it-shop wall. Me and Gracie and Grandpa watched a little red light flash on the map. Right over Hershey, Pennsylvania.

"Gracie, look," I said. I pointed. "That must be where we're going next."

"Mom and Dad are there," said Gracie. "Waiting for us." She touched her locket. The one Mom gave her.

The big wall clock said it was after midnight. That's late for me and Gracie. But we wouldn't be here long. I mean, here in Grandpa's fix-it shop way in the back of our family's museum. The Stockton Museum of Just About Everything in American History.

We're taking off to rescue our parents. In the time machine.

Taptaptap TAP—TAP—TAP taptaptap went the old telegraph.

"Sh-h-h-h, kids," Grandpa said. "Your parents are sending another message."

He sat down at the old telegraph machine. Me and Gracie ran and stood next to him.

Mom and Dad. My stomach got all jittery.

Gracie squeezed my hand.

We watched Grandpa write down the message.

"Pennsylvania . . . 1903."

"Let's go," I said. I pushed up my glasses with one finger. "We know where they are, so what are we hanging around here for?"

"You're not going anywhere," Grandpa said. He pulled two sandwiches and a small bag of potato chips out of a brown paper bag.

"Not until you eat these," he said. He handed the sandwiches and chips to me and Gracie. "Who knows how long you'll go without food once you get to Hershey."

Gracie patted Grandpa's arm. "Don't worry, Grandpa," she said. "We know what we're doing."

I tried to eat my sandwich, but I didn't feel hungry. I was afraid to travel back in time again. Swirling in a time machine is scary. My stomach gets tied in knots. My hands sweat. My eyes go all wet. I couldn't tell Gracie, though.

Because she's also braver than me.

That's the way I see it, anyway. Of course, I'll never tell *her* that. It would go straight to her head.

We *had* to go back in time to save Mom and Dad. Even if I was scared to go. They were still out there somewhere. Trapped in the past. And only Gracie and I could bring them home.

Grandpa paged through a tall stack of papers

next to the telegraph machine. "According to this, your mom and dad bought a rug from a Mr. Milton Hershey in Hershey, Pennsylvania. In 1903."

"Hershey?" I said. "Like the candy bar?" This trip was sounding better now.

Gracie rolled her eyes. "1903?" she said. "Ick. That means I'll have to wear a dress when we get there."

"I'll bring in the rug while you kids eat," Grandpa said. He left the room.

I took a bite of my sandwich. Tuna and pickles. My second favorite. I like tuna and chips best.

"Hey, Gracie. Maybe you'll get lucky and turn into a llama this time," I said. "Or an iguana. Then you can't wear a dress."

When we traveled back in time to Delaware, Gracie turned into a horse. Now *that* was funny.

Gracie put her hands on her hips. "Grow up, George," she said. "This is serious."

I crossed my eyes at her.

"Besides," she said. And then she raised one eyebrow. "Maybe you'll be the iguana this time."

"Gulp," was all I could say back. Because I hadn't thought of that. "Gulp gulp."

Grandpa came back in the room. He dragged a

rug behind him. A big red one with gold fringe on the edges.

"Whoa!" I said.

"It's huge," said Gracie.

"And heavy," said Grandpa. He dropped the rug on the floor in front of us. Dust puffed into the air. "But it's beautiful, isn't it? Too bad we can't keep it for the museum."

Gracie knelt down and stroked the rug. She sneezed again. "Mom and Dad touched this," she said.

"How will we ever get that in the time machine?" I said.

"It will fit," said Grandpa. "You'll see." He took a deep breath. "I should be the one to go back in time," he said. "Instead of you kids. It's downright dangerous the two of you going alone like this."

"But you can't go Grandpa," I said. "You've been to the past too many times already. With Mom and Dad. And you brought stuff back, like they did."

"So you could get trapped, too," Gracie said. "And then what would happen to me and George?" She touched her locket again.

"Yes, yes," said Grandpa. "I know." He looked tired.

"We'll be okay, Grandpa," I said.

I said it. But I wasn't so sure.

Crowe would be waiting for us when we landed in Pennsylvania.

For us and the time machine.

Grandpa told us not to trust Crowe. Mom and Dad warned us about him, too.

Gracie held Grandpa's hand. She was scared, too. I could tell by her face.

Then she turned to me. "Okay, George," she said. She took a deep breath. "Let's go."

I walked over to the corner where the time machine had landed after our last trip to Delaware in 1776. The time machine always changes shape when it travels. It was an outhouse in Delaware. Now it was an old trunk.

I ran my hands over the trunk. It jiggled and sort of purred. "Yep," I said. "It's awake."

The time machine seems to like me and Gracie. I guess that's a good thing.

"Why does the time machine change shape when it travels?" Gracie said. She got her scrunched-up thinking face on. It's not pretty to look at, I tell you.

"I'm not sure," said Grandpa. "But I have a theory. I think it's trying to disguise itself."

"Crowe can't steal the time machine if he doesn't know what it looks like. Right?"

"That's what I think, George," Grandpa said.

"See, Gracie?" I said. I tapped my forehead. "I keep telling you. I am the brains of the family."

Gracie snorted.

"Pay attention to what the time machine changes into when you get to Pennsylvania," Grandpa said. "You can't get back home if you can't find it. And if Crowe gets to the time machine before you do . . ."

I felt my stomach squish up.

"We'll be trapped in time, too." My stomach got tight. "With Crowe."

"You can't let that happen," said Grandpa. He put his hand on my shoulder. "Remember, Crowe has to go wherever the time machine goes. And he knows who you two are now. So take care of each other."

"We will," Gracie said. She squeezed her lips together, tight.

We all got quiet. Grandpa's worried face told me that in another minute, he wouldn't let us go. But we *had* to. Even if we were scared.

"Come on, George," Gracie said. "Let's put the rug in the trunk."

I tried to smile. "Okay, Gracie."

Gracie's got guts. That's for sure. Brave guts.

Me and Gracie pulled on the rug. We could hardly move it. Grandpa helped.

When we got the rug close to the trunk, the trunk shook and made a strange humming sound.

The lid flew open and WHOOSH! The rug disappeared inside.

I fell back into Grandpa.

Gracie fell into me.

"Cool," I said.

"That's so dangerous," said Gracie. "If we got our fingers caught in there . . ."

Grandpa shook his head. "All these years traveling with the time machine and it still surprises me," he said.

"I guess it's our turn now," Gracie said. "Ready, George?"

I wanted to say, *No way. I'm* not *going.* But I didn't.

"Yeah," I said.

Grandpa hugged us both.

"I wish you didn't have to go," he said. "Do not forget that Crowe will be waiting for you."

"Don't worry," I said. "We know who he is now.

We'll be careful."

Gracie nodded. "I'll take care of George," she said. She put her arm around me. "You know how he is."

"Yeah," I said. "Brilliant."

Grandpa smiled.

Gracie climbed into the trunk. It grew wider.

I climbed in after her. The trunk got even wider. Like a mouth.

"Ouch! You're on my ankle," Gracie said.

"Sorry," I said. I sat down and crossed my legs.

Grandpa stood back.

"This is it, Gracie," I said.

She rubbed her ankle. "I've done this before, you know," she said.

The time machine made a loud whirring sound, like a helicopter, and lit up. Two pairs of seatbelts grew out of the sides of the trunk and snapped together over our laps.

My heart flip flopped.

Gracie clutched her locket.

We stared at each other.

The whirring sound got louder and louder.

The lid on the trunk started to close.

"Be careful," Grandpa yelled.

I nodded. So did Gracie.

She reached over and took my hand.

"We'll be okay, George," she said.

Then BANG! The lid slammed shut.

And ZOOM! We were inside a black hole.

The adventure continues in . . .

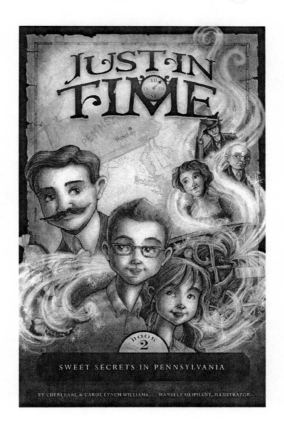

Sweet Secrets in Pennsylvania

CPSIA information can be obtained at www.ICGtesting.com
Printed in the USA
LVOW120531100413

328247LV00004B/5/P